W9-CER-947

SHARK AND LOBSTER's

Amazing Undersea Adventure

Written and drawn by
Viviane Schwarz

colored by
Joel Stewart

Text and illustrations copyright © 2006
by Silvia T. Viviane Schwarz

Coloring copyright © 2006 by Joel Stewart

"Shark's Song" is reproduced with
kind permission from the composer,
Matthew Robins.

All rights reserved. No part of this book may
be reproduced, transmitted, or stored in an
information retrieval system in any form or
by any means, graphic, electronic, or
mechanical, including photocopying,
taping, and recording, without prior
written permission from the publisher.

First U.S. edition 2006

Library of Congress Cataloging-in-
Publication Data is available.

Library of Congress Catalog Card
Number 2005050183

ISBN 0-7636-2910-3

10 9 8 7 6 5 4 3 2 1

Printed in China

The text in this book was typed on an
Oliver typewriter. The speech bubbles
were hand lettered by Viviane Schwarz.
The illustrations were drawn in ink,
then digitally colored.

Candlewick Press
2067 Massachusetts Avenue
Cambridge, Massachusetts 02140

visit us at www.candlewick.com

for Mel

V. S.

CANDLEWICK PRESS
CAMBRIDGE, MASSACHUSETTS

TIGERS!

I've HEARD of them! They walk on their TEETH, they GLOW in the DARK, and they EAT YOU UP!
Now I'm scared TOO!
you should be. Let's build a FORTRESS to keep us SAFE from tigers.
Brilliant idea!

Five minutes later,
the small cuttlefish
had fetched her family
and friends,
and her friends' families,
and some very spiky crabs.

They brought seven hundred
rocks and a piano.
Now they had walls.
The cuttlefish played the
piano, and Lobster danced
with the crabs.

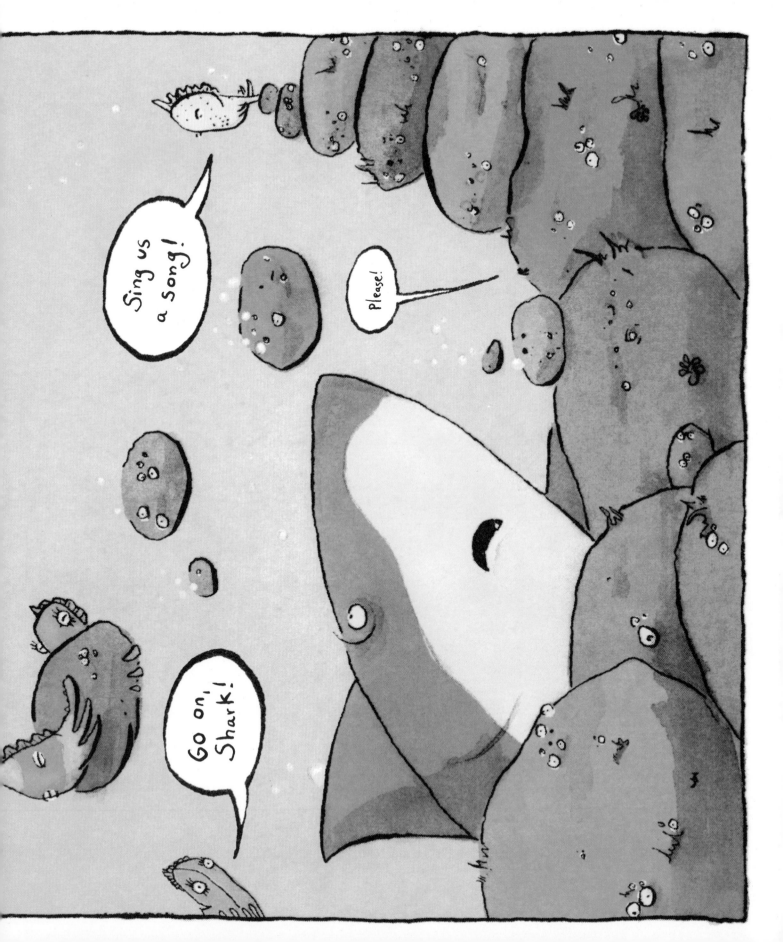

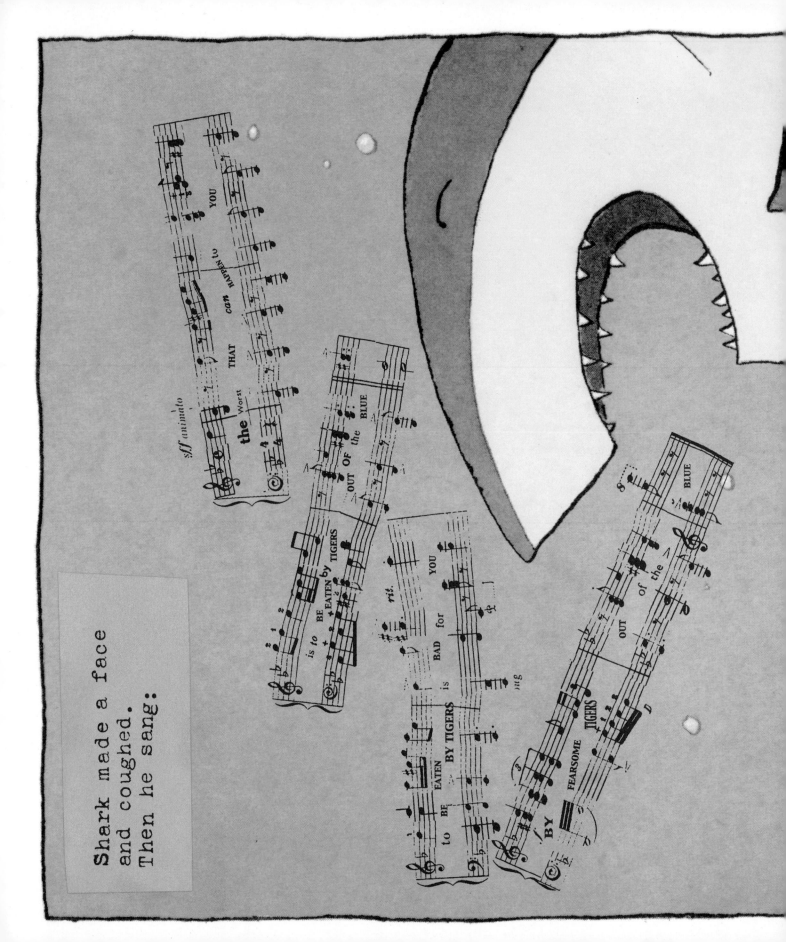

Shark made a face
and coughed.
Then he sang:

There was a great clattering as the spiky crabs shivered with fright.

Haverstraw King's Daughters Public Library

We need something BETTER to keep the tigers away. We need a TRULY FRIGHTFUL THING.
Like a HUGE BIG MONSTER from the DEEP SEA! GREAT!
Let's get a MONSTER!

So they all went
down into the
deep sea, diving
and
tumbling and
sinking.

They didn't have to look for long.
There was a huge big monster
stretched out as far as they could see.
Its mouth was wide enough to eat
a whale sideways.

LOOK at all the LEGS!
I'VE GOT EIGHT THOUSAND
AND TWO...
And look at all the EYES!
I'VE GOT SEVEN
AND A FEW...
Where's the END of it?
THE SMALLEST DOT OF LIGHT OUT IN THE DARK— THAT'S THE LANTERN ON THE END OF MY TAIL.

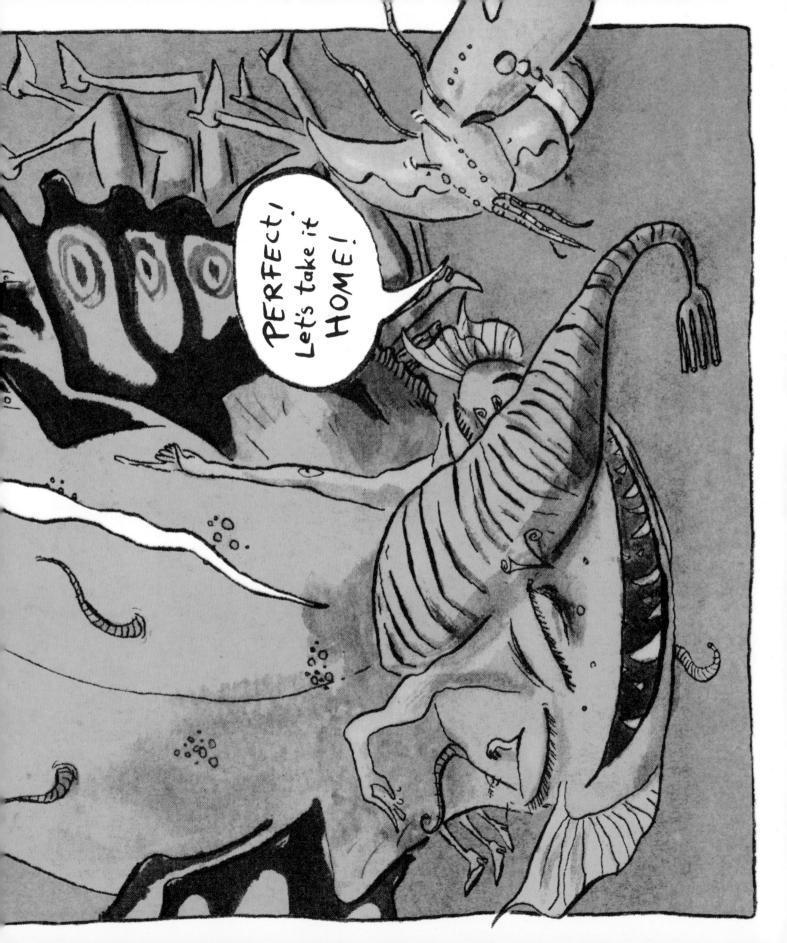

Together
they carried
the sleeping monster
up from
the deep
sea....

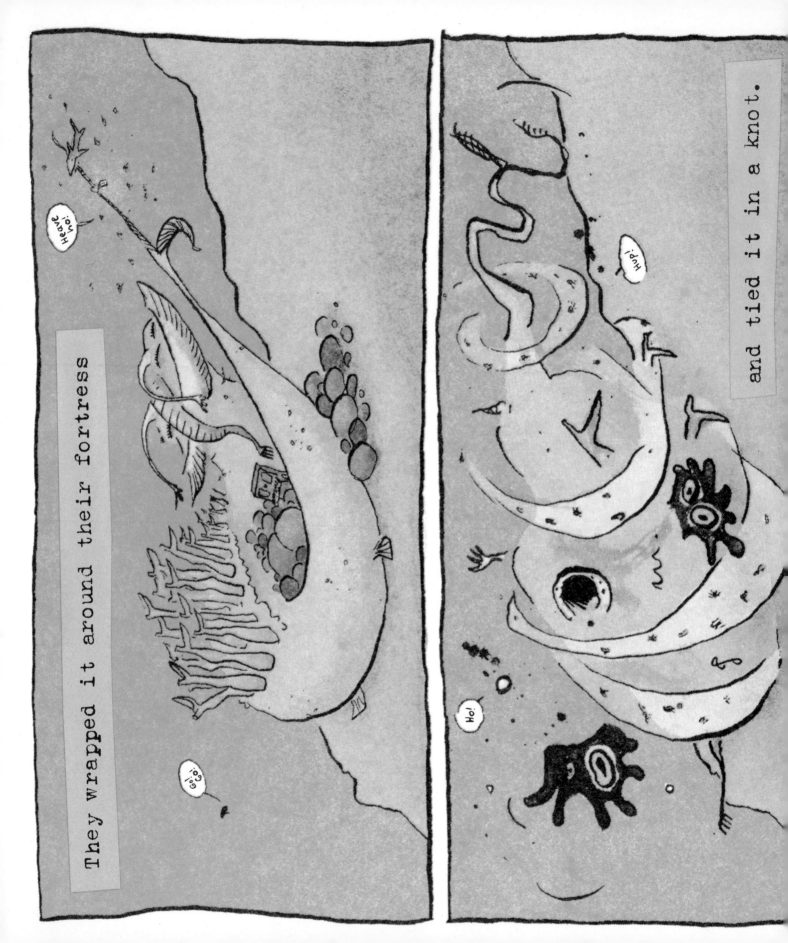

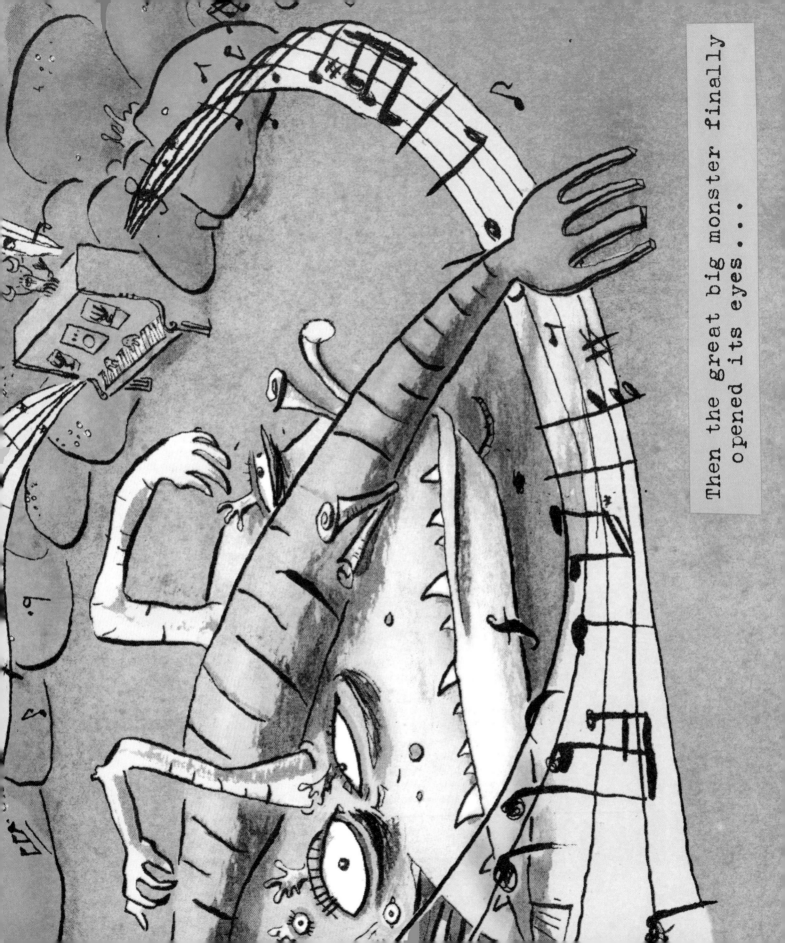

Then the great big monster finally opened its eyes. . . .

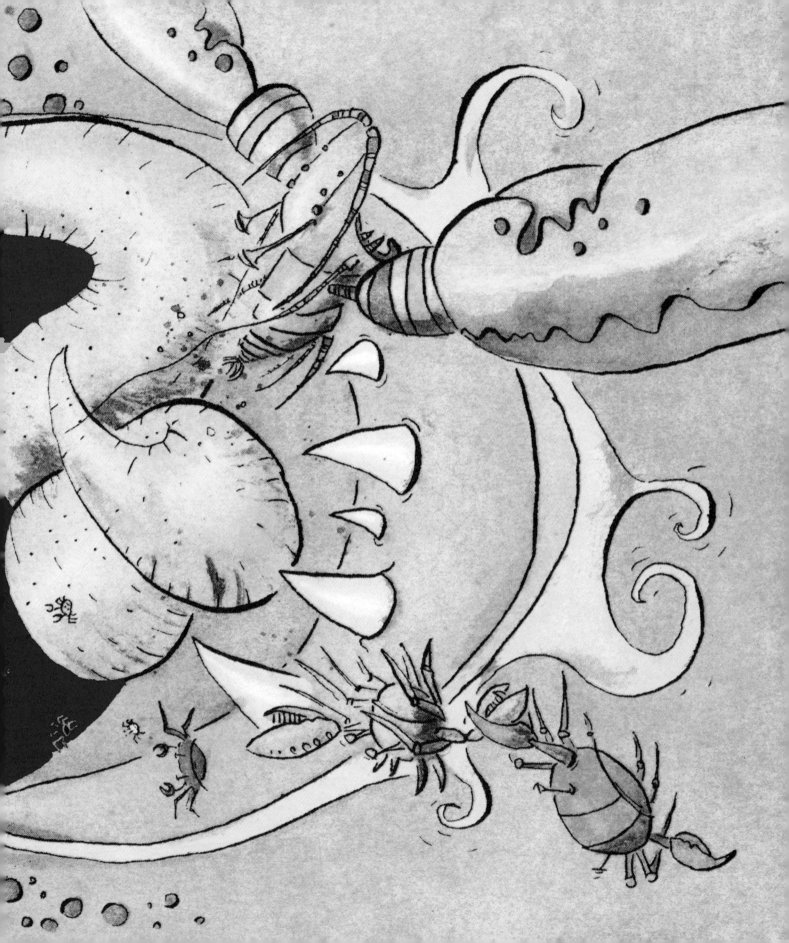

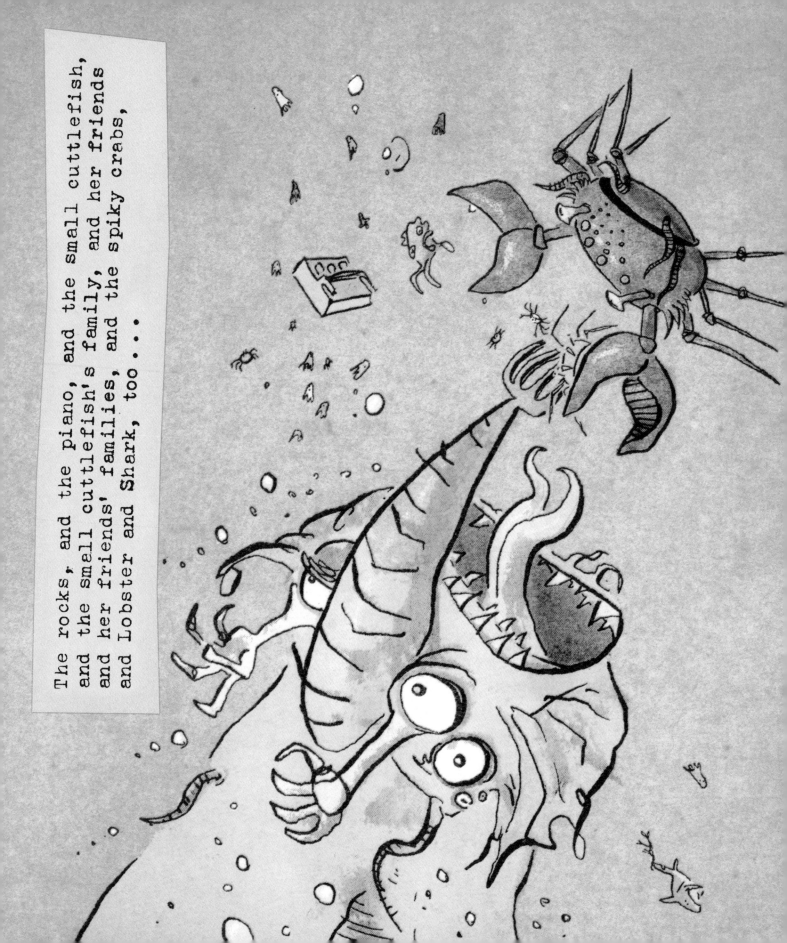

The rocks, and the piano, and the small cuttlefish, and the small cuttlefish's family, and her friends' families, and the spiky crabs, and Lobster and Shark, too. . . .

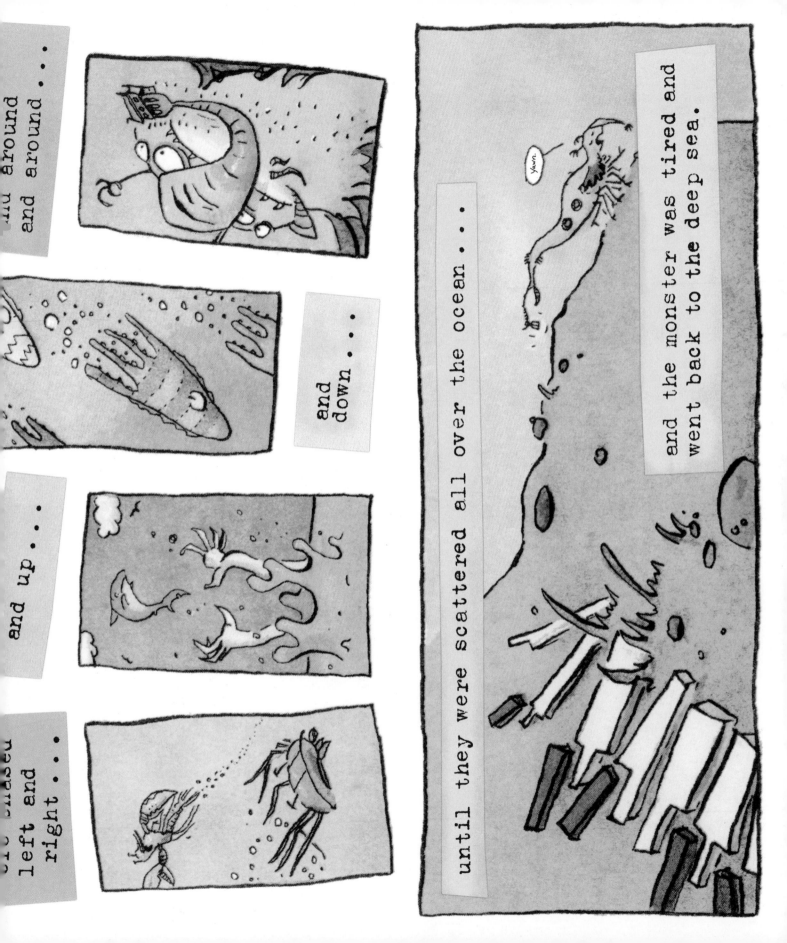

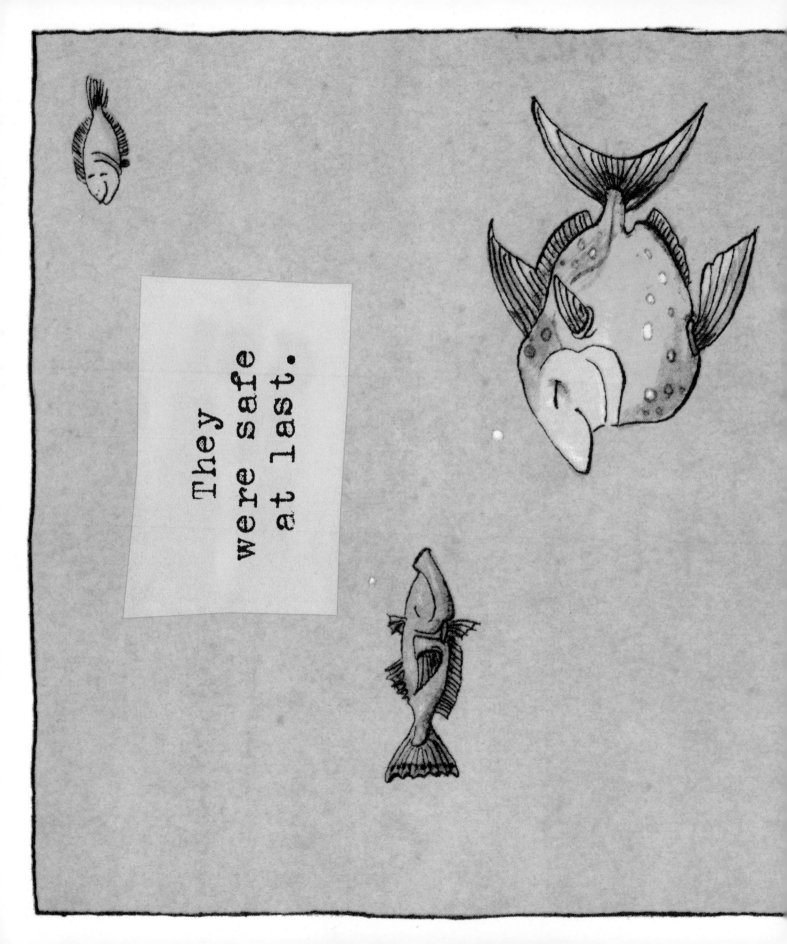

They were safe at last.

But what about TIGERS? They're full of TEETH and STRIPES!
WHO CARES? I'M full of teeth, and YOU'RE full of stripes!

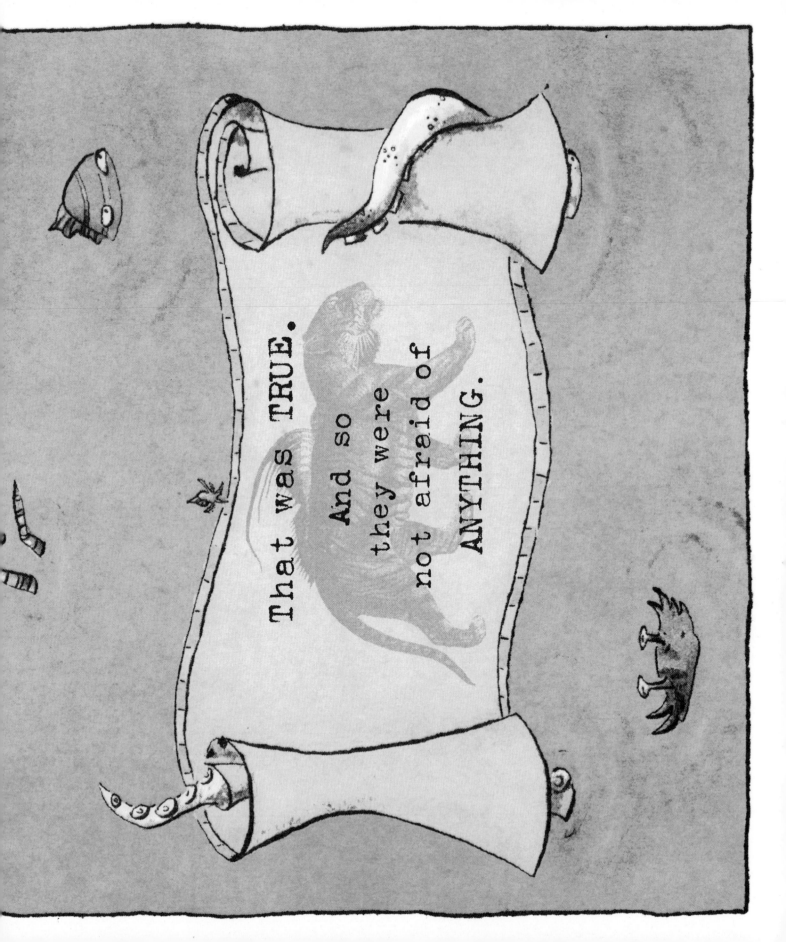